This book belongs to

_____

This edition published by Parragon Books Ltd in 2017

Parragon Books Ltd
Chartist House
15–17 Trim Street
Bath BA1 1HA, UK
www.parragon.com

Copyright © Parragon Books Ltd 2017

Illustrated by: Judi Abbot
Reading consultant: Geraldine Taylor

ISBN 978-1-4748-6311-7

Printed in China

The Three Billy Goats Gruff

PaRragon

Bath • New York • Cologne • Melbourne • Delhi
Hong Kong • Shenzhen • Singapore

Five steps for enjoyable reading

Traditional stories and fairy tales are a great way to begin reading practice. The stories and characters are familiar and lively. Follow the steps below to help your child become a confident and independent reader.

Step 1
Read the story aloud to your child. Run your finger under the words as you read.

Three goats lived on a green hillside. Little Billy Goat Gruff was small and white. Middle Billy Goat Gruff was middle-sized and brown. And Big Billy Goat Gruff was huge and grey. He had long, curly horns.

8

Step 2
Look at the pictures and talk about what is happening.

Step 3

Read the simple text on the right-hand page together. When reading, some words come up again and again, such as **the**, **to** or **and**. Your child will quickly learn to recognize these high-frequency words by sight.

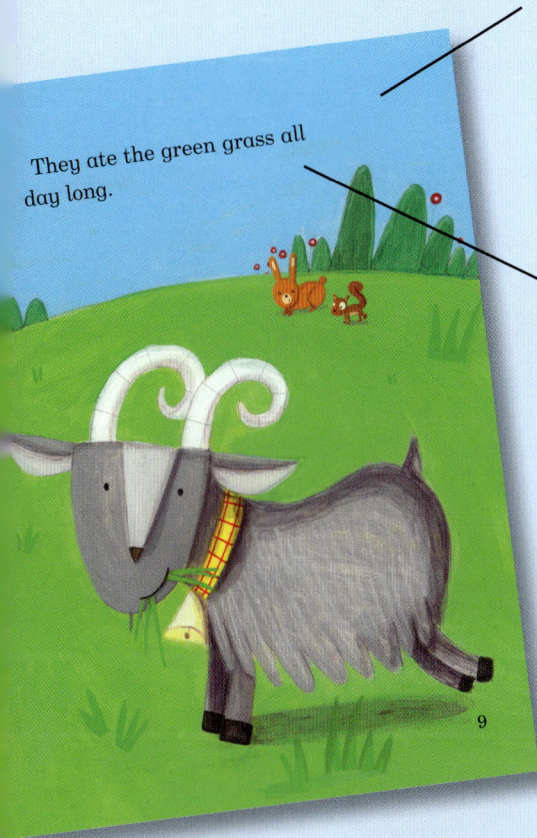

They ate the green grass all day long.

9

Step 4

When your child is ready, encourage them to read the simple lines on their own.

Step 5

Help your child to complete the puzzles at the back of the book.

Three goats lived on a green hillside.
Little Billy Goat Gruff was small and
white. Middle Billy Goat Gruff was
middle-sized and brown. And Big
Billy Goat Gruff was huge and grey.
He had long, curly horns.

They ate the green grass all day long.

One day, the three Billy Goats Gruff were hungry.

"There's no grass left here!" said Little Billy Goat Gruff in his teeny, tiny voice.

"But there's sweet green grass over there," said Middle Billy Goat Gruff.

"Let's cross over the river," said Big Billy Goat Gruff, in his great big voice.

How will they cross over
the river?

The three Billy Goats Gruff had to cross over the bridge. But under the bridge lived the Bad Old Troll.

He was hairy and scary, mean and green – with the sharpest teeth you've ever seen!

"Grrr!" he growled. "This is my bridge!"

"Oh no!" said the three Billy Goats Gruff.

The Bad Old Troll would not let
them go over the bridge.

13

Little Billy Goat Gruff was clever and brave.

"Watch me," he said to his brothers, in his teeny, tiny voice.

He trip-trap-trotted onto the bridge.

"Stop!" shouted the Troll. "Who's that trip-trapping on my bridge?"

"It's me – Little Billy Goat Gruff!"

"I will eat you!" said the Bad
Old Troll.

15

"Please don't eat me," said Little Billy Goat Gruff. "Wait for Middle Billy Goat Gruff. He's much bigger than me. There's more of him to eat!"

"Grrr. All right, you may cross," said the Bad Old Troll.

So Little Billy Goat Gruff quickly trip-trap-trotted over the bridge.

The Bad Old Troll let him go over
the bridge.

17

Next, Middle Billy Goat Gruff
trip-trap-trotted onto the bridge.

"Stop!" shouted the Troll. "Who's that
trip-trapping on my bridge?"

"It's me – Middle Billy Goat Gruff!"

"Yum! I will eat you!" said the
Bad Old Troll.

"Please don't eat me," said Middle Billy Goat Gruff. "Wait for Big Billy Goat Gruff. He's much, much bigger than me. There's more of him to eat!"

"Then you can cross over too," said
the Bad Old Troll.

At last, it was the turn of Big Billy Goat Gruff. He clip-clop-clomped onto the bridge.

"Stop!" shouted the Troll. "Who's that clip-clopping on my bridge?"

"It's me – Big Billy Goat Gruff!" said Big Billy Goat Gruff in his great big voice.

"You are big. I will eat you!" said the Bad Old Troll.

The Troll was hairy and scary, mean and green, with the sharpest teeth you've ever seen!

But Big Billy Goat Gruff wasn't scared. Oh no. He just put his head down and stamped his feet.

Then Big Billy Goat Gruff ran at the Troll with his long, curly horns.

The Troll tipped into the water!

Clip-clop-clomp went Big Billy Goat Gruff's hooves. He ran over the bridge and into the field. Soon the three Billy Goats Gruff were eating the sweet green grass all day long.

And that was the end of
the Bad Old Troll.

Puzzle time!

Which two words rhyme?

bad   can   day   tip   say

Which word does not match the picture?

brown
goat
Troll

Which words match the picture?

green
grass
gruff

Who went over the bridge last?

Big Billy Goat
Middle Billy Goat
Little Billy Goat

Which sentence is right?

The Troll tipped into the water.
The goat tipped into the water.